The Big Hike

The Big Hike

The Adventures of Dillon and Kyle

By
Dr. Dennis S. Atkinson

Illustrated by
Ray Hartland

Post Office Box 1099 • Murfreesboro, Tennessee 37133

Copyright 2003 by
Sword of the Lord Publishers
ISBN 0-87398-089-1

Printed and Bound in the United States of America

To

My beloved wife, Patricia—my silent
partner in the ministry and the person
responsible for initiating the writing
of this book.

Contents

Foreword 8

Acknowledgments 9

1. Planning Day 11

2. "Fencetracked" 23

3. Old Crackfire 37

4. Devil's Den 51

5. The Lunchtime Mishap 65

6. Crosby's Surprise 81

7. Smith's Pasture 97

8. Sherman's Woods 111

9. The Dome 127

Foreword

I consider it a great honor to be asked to write a foreword for Dr. Dennis Atkinson's first book. He is not only a great associate of mine, a good man who loves the Lord and His work, but he is an authority on how to communicate with children. I have watched him over the last several years as he has loved children and taught them the truths of God's Word. He has a way of speaking to children that is a gift from God. I hope you enjoy his work and trust the biblical principles taught will strengthen your walk with God.

DR. NORRIS E. BELCHER, JR.

Church of the Open Door
Westminster, Maryland

Acknowledgments

Special thanks to my wife, Patricia Atkinson, and my daughter, Emilee Atkinson Wiebenga, for editing and proofreading the manuscripts.

Chapter 1
Planning Day

It was Friday afternoon, school was out for the weekend, and Dillon and Kyle were sitting on the front porch of Dillon's house discussing their plans for Saturday. Both boys were eleven and had been best friends ever since they met in first grade. They had spent a lot of time together growing up and were adventurers at heart.

Dillon was the leader of the two. His brown hair sometimes looked orange for some reason. The reason it appeared orange may have had something to do with the crew cut he had or maybe the way the sun shone on it. No one could ever figure it out. The crew cut matched his squared-off nose, which supported his glasses.

Kyle was a blonde-haired boy with a mop haircut. You could always tell when he was around. His squeaky voice, always full of excitement and energy, was unmistakable and easy to recognize.

"I think we should take an all-day hike outside of town," Kyle suggested. "My dad said it was going to be a perfect fall day."

"And just what is a perfect fall day?" asked Dillon.

"Well, you know—it's cool outside, yet still warm. Kind of like some warm apple pie with ice cream on it."

"Why did you have to mention pie and ice cream?" Dillon complained in a whiny voice. "I'm hungry enough as it is!"

"Hey, since you're talking about food, we can—"

Dillon interrupted before Kyle could finish the sentence. "I wasn't talking about food; you were. And besides, I've never seen a fall day that looked like ice cream!"

Kyle laughed, "Well, you will tomorrow. It's

going to be all apple pie and ice cream. So I say we pack a lunch and go for the whole day."

"Sounds good to me. We'll pack our knapsacks and take off right after breakfast," Dillon replied.

As they sat on the big porch of the old white house, they began to make some plans. "Which way do you want to go?" Kyle asked. "Should we go through Sherman's Woods, then across to Smith's pasture?"

Dillon got a blank look on his face as he thought about it. "I've got a better idea!" he exclaimed with a burst of thought-energy. "Let's go over toward Andrea's house and take the path that leads up through Miller's Hill. Then we can go over to Devil's Den."

Devil's Den was actually just a section of rocky terrain hidden by oak trees and marked by several secret hiding places. Dillon and Kyle would often go there to play on the large rocks or to use it as a hiding place from other boys, and especially girls.

While on a trip to the Civil War battlefield in Gettysburg, Pennsylvania one summer, they saw the real Devil's Den, which looked much like their secret hiding place. It had large, smooth limestone rocks which you could climb on. The rocks looked like someone had dropped them from the sky and they had landed in a big pile.

The real Devil's Den got its name because the rocks were home to a den of rattle-snakes. The farmers tried to rid the area of these dangerous snakes. One of them was very large and hard to catch. So mean was he that they called him the Old Devil. Over the years the name stayed with the place. Dillon and Kyle liked the spooky-sounding name and began to call their hideout Devil's Den.

Kyle exclaimed, "Devil's Den is a great idea! We can sit there and take a break before we go over to Sherman's Woods. There is only one problem," he added. "I don't know where Andrea lives."

Dillon took out a piece of green paper and began to make a handmade map of their journey. He marked the way they would travel, then showed it to Kyle. He also made a map to give to his mother before they left so she would know where they were going, just in case they didn't return home on time.

14

Dillon looked over at Kyle and pointed at his map: "We'll just follow this map so we will be sure to get back home before dark. I'll give this to Mom when I get home today."

Kyle nodded in agreement. "That's a good idea."

The Big Hike

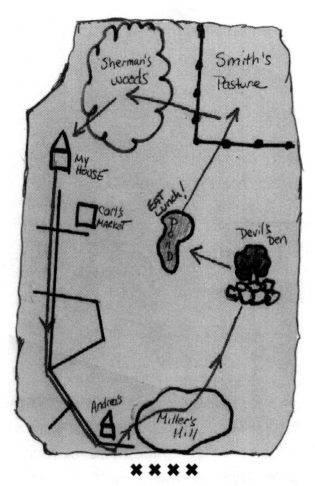

✖ ✖ ✖ ✖

How about you? Have you ever made a map? Have you ever planned a trip or a route to take for a fun afternoon like Dillon and Kyle did?

They are about to have some great adventures in the day ahead. I can hardly wait to share them with you. But before I do, let me ask you a question: What about your future? Wouldn't it be a good idea to plan your future instead of just wandering through life not knowing where you will end up?

To plan your future, you need to have a map. Just like Dillon and Kyle made a map for their trip, you ought to make a map of your life's journey. Keep in mind that there are some paths that are safe and some that are dangerous. God helps us understand the safe places in life, as well as the dangerous ones, by placing instruction in the Bible. In fact, Proverbs, chapter 3, is a tremendous chapter to help you plan a map for your future.

Let me share with you some good advice to keep in mind as you plan your future.

Plan your life according to God's map of life—the Word of God. Here are two reasons you should do this:

First, God's will is your safest route. A good map is made according to existing routes and paths. In life, God can give you the safest routes because He is the one who designed you. He is the one who knows your future long before you will ever live it.

God has established routes and paths for you to take that will be best for you. Look at Proverbs 2:6–9:

"For the LORD giveth wisdom: out of his mouth cometh knowledge and understanding.

"He layeth up sound wisdom for the righteous: he is a buckler to them that walk uprightly.

"He keepeth the paths of judgment, and preserveth the way of his saints.

"Then shalt thou understand righteousness, and judgment, and equity; yea, every good path."

In other words, God is the source of wisdom, knowledge and understanding. If you will follow His Word, you can be assured that it is the best advice. He says that He will be your "buckler." That was a means of defense used by the soldiers in Old Testament times. The soldiers would take their large shields and form a wall around themselves. It was like a portable fort.

God says He will preserve your way and show you the right paths to travel in your life ahead—not paths like Dillon and Kyle will be walking on, but paths which will help you know what you will do as you grow older.

Second, God's will is your happiest route. Proverbs 4:18,19 says this:

"But the path of the just is as the shining light, that shineth more and more unto the perfect day.

"The way of the wicked is as darkness: they know not at what they stumble."

For the Christian boys and girls living for God, the days can be happy ones. This is what God means when He says the path is "as the shining light." Life can be full of direction from God and be filled with happy times.

This doesn't mean that every day will be perfect. It doesn't mean that there will be no days of tears and difficulty. But it does mean that you can be happy even in the darkest of times.

19

The Big Hike

The wicked, or those who don't live for God, have one day after another filled with darkness and misery. They stumble and fall in life and make wrong decisions which lead to more unhappiness.

 How can we know if we are following God's map of life? Proverbs 3:1-4 tells us three ways we can be sure of this:

Number one, by not forgetting the Law of God.

"My son, forget not my law; but let thine heart keep my commandments."

The Bible word "forget" has the idea of mislaying something and not remembering where you put it. We should not carelessly mislay God's map of life and forget to apply those principles and commandments to our daily duties.

Number two, by keeping the commandments of God. The Hebrew word for "keep" is just the opposite of the word "forget." It means to keep guard on the commandments of God. Rather than be careless, we are to be responsible in applying God's Word in our future and in our daily life.

Number three, by not forgetting the mercy and truth of God. The Bible tells you to "bind them about thy neck."

Girls like to place beautiful and valued necklaces around their necks and close to their hearts. In the same way, we are to place God's Word in our lives. We are to treasure it and keep it close to our hearts. We are not to forget God's mercy and the truth of His Word.

Why don't you right now pray and ask God to help you follow His Word throughout your life? Why don't you right now make a decision to follow the paths of God?

✖ ✖ ✖ ✖

Now it's time to get back to the story. Dillon and Kyle went home and began to pack and prepare for the big hike. They packed food, extra clothes and anything else they thought would help them through the journey. Most importantly, they packed their Bibles.

As they went to bed that evening, they had a hard time getting to sleep as the thoughts of adventure ran through their heads. But they rested well because they knew God would be with them each step of the way.

Chapter 2
"Fencetracked"

The sun was shining over the small, friendly town when Saturday arrived, just as the weatherman had forecast. The boys were up, ready and standing on the porch of Dillon's house. It was warming up quite nicely, and it was truly the perfect day for their hike.

"Do you have the map?" asked Kyle.

"Yes! I have it right here in my pocket," assured Dillon as he patted his pocket with his hand. "Let's see," he went on, "we decided to go past Andrea's house and on to Miller's Hill."

Dillon and Kyle gathered up their things, put on the knapsacks with lots of snacks and some sandwiches and made sure their canteens were full of water. And of course they were bringing along some cake that Kyle's mother had made the day before.

"Well, let's go," Kyle said eagerly as he started to walk down the sidewalk. Dillon was quickly spurred into action. They were as excited as two boys could be at the ripe old age of eleven, and now their journey had begun, but it quickly took an unexpected turn.

As Dillon and Kyle rounded the corner just a few blocks away from Dillon's house, they noticed a school chum named José across the street.

"Hey, guys, wait up!" José called out. They waited until he crossed the street. Dillon and Kyle had begun to walk as José trotted to catch up to them.

"Where are you going with all that stuff?" José asked as he pointed to the knapsacks.

"On a hike," answered Dillon reluctantly.

"Yeah, and we're going alone," added Kyle. Kyle wasn't usually so rude, but they had waited so long for this trip, they didn't want any more delays.

The boys showed him the map and

"Fencetracked"

explained to José what they were doing, as they hiked to the edge of town. In fact, Andrea's house was dead ahead, and the path to Miller's Hill was just beyond.

"You don't want to go that way. It will

take too long. Besides, your map isn't right," José asserted with a wrinkled-up expression, implying how silly their thinking was.

Dillon was showing some doubt in his face as he pondered José's comment. "But I checked this out with my dad. He knows this town and said this was a good way to go."

"Ah, you ought to know better than to believe your dad. He'll send you in the *safest* direction possible." Of course, José said this with sarcasm, just to poke fun at Dillon. "After all, he doesn't want his little 'Dilly' to get hurt. But I know a way that would be really fun. Whole lots better than that dumb old Devil's Den you're going to. You guys follow me. I know a really great place to explore," José said convincingly.

José started walking away from Andrea's house and back towards Dillon's. Dillon and Kyle looked at each other with a look that said, *What do you think we should do?*

José stopped and turned around. "Well, are you guys coming, or are you going to that stupid Devil's Pen?" he shouted mockingly as he emphasized the 'Pen' part of the name.

"Fencetracked"

Dillon and Kyle didn't quite know why, but soon they were following José down the street. They crossed through town until they came upon some woods behind the run-down grocery store called Carl's Market. It had been there since their parents were kids. José pointed to a path that was barely visible that went between two big bushes. "It's right here," he said as he pushed the bushes apart.

"What's right here?" Kyle hesitantly asked.

José just kept walking and replied mysteriously, "You'll see! But you need to walk slowly and quietly from here on out."

Dillon and Kyle were a little nervous when he said this, but neither admitted it. They didn't want to be "fraidy cats," as José would have liked to call them. So they just kept walking slowly and quietly through the dark woods.

José kept looking from side to side as if he were looking for someone. As they came to the edge of the woods, Kyle and Dillon could see a chain-link fence with a wooden gate rising high above them. José pointed to

it and whispered, "There it is!"

Kyle questioned José: "What is? I don't see anything but a fence! You mean, you brought us up here to look at a fence?"

"Not the fence, dummy! It's what's beyond it. All we have to do is climb this fence, and we are in. But we have to hurry before someone sees us!" he said in a hurried whisper.

Dillon and Kyle couldn't help noticing the

big yellow sign with black letters.

No Trespassing

Keep Out

Violators Will Be Prosecuted

"I don't like this," protested Kyle.

"We can be arrested if we cross over that fence," added Dillon.

"You guys are a bunch of 'fraidy cats'! They won't do anything to us, and besides, no one is here right now," José said with a tough-sounding, confident voice.

"Then why are we being so quiet?" asked Kyle.

"I did that to scare you. It was a joke. Now are you coming, or aren't you?" he asked with a dare.

It was then that Dillon remembered a passage of Scripture in Proverbs 3:5–8 that he had learned in Sunday school the previous week.

✖ ✖ ✖ ✖

Before we continue with the story, let me ask you what you think Dillon and Kyle should do. This is what Proverbs 3:5-8 says:

"*Trust in the* L*ORD* *with all thine heart; and lean not unto thine own understanding.*

"*In all thy ways acknowledge him, and he shall direct thy paths.*

"*Be not wise in thine own eyes: fear the* L*ORD, and depart from evil.*

"*It shall be health to thy navel, and marrow to thy bones.*"

Three commands found in these verses will keep you from getting sidetracked or, as in the situation of Dillon and Kyle, "fence-tracked."

First, trust in the Lord. There is only one Person in whom we should place all of our trust—the Lord Jesus Christ. Yes, we can trust our parents to do their best, but only Jesus will *never* fail you.

We are to trust the Lord with all our hearts, not just part of them. We should not trust God just until something else comes along.

As the boys were making their decisions, they needed to decide what they would do based upon what God would want them to do. Instead, they listened to what José said as he led them away from their plan.

When others try to turn your direction away from God and the right path, stick to the map of God's will and trust what He has told you to do.

The boys also shifted their trust from their original plan to José's plan. However, the final decision was theirs. They couldn't place the blame upon José. They had kept God out of their plan altogether and trusted in their own judgment.

The problem with trusting in our own judgment is that we do not know the future. It is easy for us to make mistakes, but God, who is perfect, makes no mistakes.

Do you have a decision to make? Do you think God wants to direct you? Of course He does! So the first thing you should keep in mind is to trust the Lord Jesus with all your heart.

Second, acknowledge God in your actions. To acknowledge God simply means that you should take notice of Him in what you are doing and make Him part of it. It is not until we acknowledge God that He will 'direct our paths.' When we go down a path, we should acknowledge God in it. We can either make our own decisions or let God make our decisions for us.

God wants us to consider Him in our decision making. No matter what that decision is, ask God to help you. That is why it says, "In *all* thy ways," not "*some of* thy ways."

As we observe God and learn about Him, we learn what He would have us do. Don't do something you are unsure about. If you don't know what God would do, then ask someone who knows.

If we seek God's will, His promise is that He will direct us. If you trust Him to know what is best and act upon what you know from God, then you will find God's direction.

We don't need a special sign or voice from Heaven. The best place to go to know about God is His Word. It has the answers for life's direction.

Third, fear the Lord. The meaning of the word "fear" is not the same as someone's being afraid of ghosts or monsters. It has the idea of respect. Respect God enough to listen to what He says.

✖ ✖ ✖ ✖

If you recall, José was asking Dillon and Kyle, "Are you coming, or aren't you?" The more they thought about it, the more they realized what José was about to do was wrong. Proverbs 3:5-8 helped them realize they should avoid evil.

They also realized that they should have never left their original path. They should have followed their map. Now they were thirty minutes behind schedule and about to use poor judgment. They were about to trust their own wisdom and not God's wisdom.

"I'm not going to climb that fence, and I don't care what you think! It's a dumb idea. Come on, Kyle. Let's head back to Andrea's like we planned," commanded Dillon.

Kyle felt relieved and agreed and quickly turned on his heels. Both were soon walking back into the woods. They looked back and could see José standing with his hands on his hips and with a look of disgust. Then he called out at them, "Fraidy cats! Fraidy cats!"

As they approached Andrea's house, they could see the path leading to Miller's Hill. Soon they were on their way up the path that led through the long, grassy hill.

"Fencetracked"

Miller's Hill was the highest point in town, and you could see for miles around when you stood at the top. Already they could see their houses and the local grocery store. They also noticed the farms that stretched out as far as they could see. Still, they kept walking upward. As they neared the crest of the hill, they noticed another dirt path leading off to the right.

"I wonder where this goes," Kyle said with a puzzled look on his face.

"I don't know," answered Dillon. "Why don't we go down the path a short way and find out?"

"Okay," agreed Kyle. "Let's go!"

Chapter 3
Old Crackfire

The path the boys were taking led through some high pasture grass that hadn't been mowed for years. It was beginning to turn a golden brown due to the autumn weather. The grass was so long that it just lay flat on the ground.

It seemed odd that the field would lie idle with no one mowing it or using it. Still, it didn't take away from the beauty of Miller's Hill.

The sun was shining, and there was a nice fall breeze as they began to go down the hill on the path before them. Looking over to their right, they could see farm after farm with their silver and blue silos. Spotted cattle grazed on the rich pastures, and neat white fences lined the boundaries of the properties.

The pasture through which they were hiking had a white fence all around it, but it had not been painted for some time, and many of the boards were broken. The narrow path wound around to the left. They trekked along about a quarter of a mile until they came to an opening through tall, untrimmed bushes. From there, the path led to a stone driveway overgrown with grass from lack of use. Tree branches lay on the ground from past summer storms.

Kyle shot Dillon a questioning glance and asked, "Should we keep on going? It doesn't look like anyone uses this land anymore."

"I don't see why we can't go on. I don't see any signs that say we can't. And if we see someone, we'll just turn around and leave," answered Dillon.

As they walked farther down the driveway, they could see an unkempt house at the end. The paint had all but worn off the sides, which gave it a dreary appearance.

As they kept on walking, they noticed a shelter of large maple trees that surrounded the house. The shrubs climbed high up the sides, and the flowerbeds were full of weeds. It appeared that no one was living there.

"Let's go up on the porch," suggested Dillon. "Maybe we can peek through the window to see if anyone is still using it." Dillon took the lead, with Kyle close on his heels.

"Look at those old, torn screens," said

Kyle with a wrinkled-up nose.

"Yeah, and the paint on this place is a mess! It doesn't look like anyone has painted it for a thousand years!"

Dillon went up to the spider-webbed windows and peeked inside. "Man, this place really is a mess! They need a housekeeper 'big time,'" he whispered.

Kyle put his nose close to the glass. "Look at the furniture. It looks like it's being used," he said in a serious tone.

"Hey, what if someone is hurt inside? Maybe some old person is in there and can't get help!" Dillon suggested.

"Or worse yet," said Kyle nervously, "maybe someone died in there. I once heard about a man who died in his house and wasn't found for a year; then he was nothing but a pile of bones."

"Really?" said Dillon as he coaxed him for more information.

"Yes-sir-ee! They found him on the rocking chair. He had died right there, and nobody knew it," exclaimed Kyle.

Now the boys were really concerned and just a little leery of doing any more investigating. However, their curiosity got the better of them. Before they knew it, Dillon was turning the doorknob to see if the door would open. Sure enough, the door was not locked. It creaked on its hinges as he slowly opened it. With the door fully opened, they slipped into the dark room.

"This looks like the living room. I don't see anyone. Let's check out the other rooms," said Dillon.

Kyle was praying they wouldn't find anyone dead in a chair, or even hurt and needing help.

They slowly tiptoed through the dingy living room. The tension could be felt in the air, and their hearts pounded in their chests.

Dillon turned to Kyle, "You open this one," he commanded in a quiet whisper. Dillon had found it hard enough to unlatch the front door; he didn't have the courage to open another one.

Kyle slowly reached for the doorknob and

began to turn it. He pushed it open a crack because he just knew that he would find a skeleton reading a book or something! Peeking into the room and looking around, he noticed that it was a den with lots of old books neatly lined up on shelves. He opened wide the door but saw only dust and cobwebs.

"It doesn't look like anyone has been in here for a while," said Kyle in his normal voice. He was feeling a little more confident, now that the place appeared to be empty. When he backed up a step so he could close the door, he bumped into a warm body. It was Dillon.

"Watch where you're going!" Dillon scolded.

They started to wheel around on their heels to go back into the living room when someone shouted from behind them, "What are you doing in here?"

They jumped in fright and both let out a scream: "Ah-h-h-h!"

An old man who looked like a hermit glared down at them with an angry look on his face. The double-barreled shotgun in his hands was pointed right at them. He looked like he was about two hundred years old. His face was unshaven; his clothes, worn out and dirty. They were certain that if they moved one inch he would fill them full of lead buckshot!

"A dead man was looking for us," said Dillon, his voice shaking with fear. "I mean, we were

looking for a dead man, and we thought a skeleton was in here!" He was so nervous that he didn't know what he was saying.

"Do I look like a skeleton?" the old hermit angrily asked as he shook the barrel around in a circular motion.

"N-n-n-o," answered Kyle. "And you're not dead either!" he added.

"No, but *you're* going to be if I shoot you with 'Old Crackfire' here," he said with a voice so rough the boys wondered if he had shot someone before. Old Crackfire was what the hermit called his shotgun, and it didn't seem like Old Crackfire was something with which you wanted to tangle.

"Now tell me what you're doing in my house before I let loose with some of Crackfire's fire!" he demanded.

"We thought maybe someone was sick or had died. We thought maybe someone needed help. So we came in to look around. Honest, mister, we didn't mean to steal anything or to do anything wrong," answered Dillon in an apologetic manner.

"Why didn't you knock first?" asked the old man gruffly.

"I guess we didn't think about it. We just thought that maybe this place was abandoned or someone was dead, so we forgot all about knocking. Please, we're sorry! We won't do it again. We promise," pleaded Kyle. Dillon was standing motionless except for his head that was nodding up and down in fervent agreement.

The old man didn't budge and just kept pointing the shotgun at them. "Well, I'll let you go this time, but don't you go snooping around my house again. Do you hear me? You could have been shot or hurt around this old house. The next time me and Old Crackfire find you in my house, we might not be so nice!"

Dillon and Kyle were thinking that if this was being *nice,* they would hate to see the man and his gun not so *nice.*

"We promise," they both agreed at the same time.

The boys began to walk quickly backwards toward the front door. As soon as their feet hit the porch, they took off running. Not bothering to look back at the old house, they ran down the driveway, then up the pathway between the bushes, and kept running until they got to the top of Miller's Hill.

When they reached the very top, they just plopped down on the ground and held their chests. Their hearts were beating a mile a minute, and they tried to catch their breath. They didn't say a word; they just sat there panting.

✖ ✖ ✖ ✖

Boys and girls, Dillon and Kyle learned this important lesson that day: *chastening* and *correction* have a purpose.

What are *chastening* and *correction*? Let's take a look.

The word "chastening" means to warn or scold someone who is doing wrong. The Bible tells us in Proverbs 3:11 that we are to *"despise not the chastening of the* LORD*; neither be weary of his correction."*

The hermit scolded the boys for being in his house without permission. Have you ever been scolded? If so, you remember how it hurt. It may not hurt physically, but it does hurt your feelings and your conscience. When we do wrong, God chastens us through the Holy Spirit and His Word. He convicts or makes us feel bad for doing wrong.

When your parents chasten you, it may include a spanking. God commands them to do that for your good. Although it is not very much fun, God tells you not to "despise" it. In other words, don't fight against it. Accept it as from the Lord Jesus.

Hebrews 12:11 says,

"Now no chastening for the present seemeth to be joyous, but grievous: nevertheless afterward it yieldeth the peaceable fruit of righteousness unto them which are exercised thereby."

Be thankful that your parents love you enough to chasten you. They want you to live a godly life. Be grateful that God loves you and wants to correct you before you get into worse sins that can harm you even more.

There is another thing we need to learn. God tells us not to grow tired of His correction. Correction is the teaching you receive from the scolding. Usually you don't just get punished; you also get instruction. You are told why the sin was wrong and how it can hurt you and others.

God corrects us through the Bible, our Book of instructions and warnings. When the hermit corrected Dillon and Kyle, they admitted their wrongdoing and asked for forgiveness. They accepted the correction and therefore learned from it.

Sometimes boys and girls react opposite of the way Dillon and Kyle did. They rebel against chastening and correction. We must always keep in mind that our sinful nature fights against doing the right thing. We have a heart that fights against authority. Satan uses our sinful nature to his advantage. He wants to hurt us. Therefore, God instructs us not to despise or grow tired of chastening and correction.

✖ ✖ ✖ ✖

As you might remember, Dillon and Kyle were sitting on the ground, and as soon as they got their hearts and breathing back to normal, they began to reflect on their frightening adventure.

Old Crackfire

"I hope we don't run into that old hermit again, don't you?" asked Dillon.

"Boy, I'll say," replied Kyle with a chuckle. "In fact, I don't care if I ever see Old Crackfire again, either. I think we had better get going."

"Our next stop is Devil's Den," said Dillon. "Maybe our hideout will be a lot less dangerous and a whole bunch more fun," he added with a hopeful voice.

They picked themselves up off the ground and were soon walking down the hill that led to their favorite place. Certainly, they would not run into any problems there. Would they?

Chapter 4
Devil's Den

The boys walked quietly down Miller's Hill and took in all the colorful scenery of God's creation. It was a spectacular sight, one that caused them to reflect on the beauty of their little town. It was as if it were tucked away in an ocean of endless fields and pastures, a sight that would linger in their minds for years to come.

When they finally reached the bottom of Miller's Hill, they came upon a white, weathered fence that they had seen before. There were upright posts connected by two horizontal boards, one at the top and one at the bottom. Two other boards formed an X from one post to the other. The fence stretched along the bottom of the hill and separated the two farms.

A small path led to an A-shaped crossover ladder made of the same white boards. Apparently, the farmer used it to cross over from one pasture to the other, and that's how it got its name. The crossover made it easier for Dillon and Kyle, since they had all that stuff to carry on their backs.

"I'm starting to get hungry," said Kyle as they trotted forward.

"Me too! In fact, I'm so hungry I think I can smell that cake Mom made for us," Dillon chuckled. "When we get to Devil's Den, why don't we take a snack break?"

"My stomach thinks that's a great idea," Kyle said with a laugh.

They marched along the pasture path, which was now beginning to be dotted with gray and white limestone rocks protruding out of the ground. This meant that Devil's Den was just ahead, for it was made up of the same type of rocks, only twenty feet taller!

"There's Devil's Den!" exclaimed Dillon.

Devil's Den

"Good. I'm so hungry I could eat my whole lunch right now!" said Kyle.

They found their way to the large pile of rocks. All around were huge pin oak and silver maple trees. It was like a fortress hidden from the rest of the world, a place where they could get away from other friends and hide. Many of their friends had heard both of them talk about this place, but they didn't know where it was. It was Dillon and Kyle's best-kept secret.

A narrow passage led between some of the huge boulders. Although it would have been very difficult for adults to squeeze through it, the small boys were able to slip through without a problem. From there, a small cavelike passageway led to an opening inside the rocks.

The denlike hideaway was like a big nest, except it was made of limestone rocks. The opening was about twenty feet in diameter and allowed them plenty of room to rest. With the trees hiding the big rocks, no one would know they were there unless he entered the woods.

"Break out the cake," said Kyle. "I'll get us a couple of sodas."

Dillon loosened the straps on his knapsack and opened the top flap. He rooted around until he found the package of cake wrapped in shiny tinfoil. Carefully he unwrapped the tinfoil so as not to get the tasty white icing stuck on it. After all, that was the best part! He took one piece and gave it to Kyle and kept the other for himself. Each took a big bite.

"Wow! This is great!" raved Kyle, his voice muffled because of the cake stuffed in his mouth. Dillon nodded his head in agreement, then swallowed another bite.

They soon finished the cake and soda.

When Dillon put his soda can down at his side, a rock caught his attention because it was so smooth and flat.

"Hey, Kyle, look at this rock," he said as he leaned over to look closer. Except for a small portion sticking out of the ground, it was entirely covered with newly fallen leaves.

Dillon scooped some of the leaves out of the way with his hands.

"It looks like there is writing on it," Kyle said, brushing aside more of the dirt and leaves. "Somebody took a knife and scratched something on it. It reads:

osep   Aydt—1796."

"What in the world does 'osep Aydt' mean?" questioned Dillon with the inquisitive look of a detective. "It doesn't make sense. Scoop some more of the dirt away."

"Wait a minute. The first word is 'Joseph.' It says:

Joseph Aydt—1796, age 17."

"It must be the name of someone who etched his name on it in the year 1796," Dillon said with a serious tone.

"And look! Below that is another name. Rub

some of that dirt away!" Kyle said as he intensely examined the stone. It said:

Eberhard Aydt—1825, age 11.

"And look here, Kyle, another name under that one. It reads:

Gus Kessler—1864, age 12."

"That one would be during the time of the Civil War!" Kyle marveled at the thought of it. "These are names of kids our age that must have come here and hid out just like us. Are there any other names?" Kyle asked.

"I don't know, but let's dig some more," Dillon said as he began to dig away more of the dirt.

"I don't see any more names. That means this has been hidden for over one hundred years, and we are the first ones to find it!" Kyle went on to surmise. "We have found a treasure that has been hidden for all these years. Those kids must have found the rock too and then etched their names on it."

The boys couldn't believe what they had found. They had been coming to Devil's Den for years but had never noticed that rock before. It had been there for hundreds of years, but only a few boys had discovered it. They now had to decide what to do with it.

✖ ✖ ✖ ✖

Before I tell you what they did, let me share with you how this story reminds me of Proverbs 3:13–16:

"Happy is the man that findeth wisdom, and the man that getteth understanding.

"For the merchandise of it is better than the merchandise of silver, and the gain thereof than fine gold.

"She is more precious than rubies: and all the things thou canst desire are not to be compared unto her.

"Length of days is in her right hand; and in her left hand riches and honour."

The Bible tells us that God's Word is a treasure. And just like the discovery that Dillon and Kyle made, boys and girls like you are still finding exciting things in the Bible.

You may be asking, "How valuable is God's Word?" God says that it is worth more than the profit of "merchandise," money you receive from working a job or from getting an allowance. Imagine having a piggy bank full of quarters, dimes and nickels. God is telling us that the Bible is far more valuable and important than that.

You see, part of the treasure from God's Word is eternal life in Heaven. From reading the Bible, we can learn how to go to Heaven when we die. Another treasure is learning how to live a happy life down here.

God also tells us that this Bible is far more valuable than gold, silver and rubies.

People do all they can to get rich. Many have died trying to get wealth. But God wants us to know that we should make the same effort to apply His Word in our daily lives as treasure seekers do in seeking gold and jewels.

Appropriate jewelry can be attractive, but God can make you *spiritually* attractive when you live like He wants you to live.

If you were to take the wealth of the richest person on earth and compare it to the value of the Bible, God says that even that much wealth could not compare to His Word.

Many people try to replace living by God's

standard with other things, like pleasure, money, education, friends, drugs, cigarettes and liquor. God is telling us here that nothing you try to replace living for Him with will ever measure up.

You need to learn how important the Bible is and why it is important to find out what it teaches. God gives us four rewards as godly treasure when we follow His Word.

First, true happiness. True happiness is a life filled with contentment in one's circumstances. It is knowing that you are under the watch care of God. If you are doing God's will to the best of your ability, then He will guide your steps. Even when you make a mistake, He can turn it around and make something good come of it.

Second, length of days. In other words, you can live longer. God has an appointed time when you will leave this earth. You can live your full time if you obey Him. Some people die before they would have because of playing with sin. Some die from drugs, alcohol, cigarettes or other things that result in a shorter life.

Third, promised riches. By following God's

principles of hard work and integrity, we can provide for our families. Then there are future riches in Heaven. As we serve the Lord, God will reward our labors. He tells us in Proverbs 8:18-21 that eternal wealth comes only from God.

"Riches and honour are with me; yea, durable riches and righteousness.

"My fruit is better than gold, yea, than fine gold; and my revenue than choice silver.

"I lead in the way of righteousness, in the midst of the paths of judgment:

"That I may cause those that love me to inherit substance; and I will fill their treasures."

Fourth, promised honor. This means that although we are sinners, we will be respected by friends and honored by God. Wow! We are considered by God to have worth and value.

Just like Dillon and Kyle, you have a great treasure right at your fingertips waiting to be discovered. You need only to open up the Bible and find it. However, the greatest treasure of all is that of eternal life with God. Do you have it?

✖ ✖ ✖ ✖

Dillon and Kyle decided to leave the rock right where it had been for hundreds of years. They also believed that the other adventurers who had left it would have wanted them to add their names to the rock. So they took out a pocketknife and etched their names onto the rock.

Dillon Holecheck, Oct. 2003, age 11

Kyle Keyser, Oct. 2003, age 11

They believed that the others who placed their names on the rock must have felt the same way that they did as they carved the letters into the stone. Dillon and Kyle could feel a sense of oneness with them. Although the boys of the past did not know them, they had wanted to keep this treasure alive. Those same boys had also found a hiding place at Devil's Den.

"I wonder if anyone else will find this rock in years ahead," pondered Dillon.

"I hope so," said Kyle. "Maybe in a hundred years another boy will happen to find this rock and place his name on it. I wonder who it will be and if it will be as exciting for him as it is for us."

They made plans to come back with a camera and take pictures of themselves standing by the rock. But for now, they would relish their great discovery, a discovery they would keep to themselves, just like the other boys probably had.

Chapter 5
The Lunchtime Mishap

Devil's Den was now distantly behind the boys, and they were making their way to eat lunch near the community pond and park. It was a pretty place to visit, with wildlife, trees of every kind, ducks and lots of other water-fowl. They would be sure to have a nice lunch there, and hopefully it would not be too crowded. They wanted their hike to remind them of the old frontier days when Daniel Boone walked alone on the Pennsylvania mountain ridges. The very thought of his outdoor adventures inspired their imaginations.

Dillon asked Kyle, "Did you ever think about what it was like in Daniel Boone's day? I just

wonder what it would have been like to face all of those Indians and wild animals!"

"I read a book that said that the local Indians made friends with Daniel Boone when he was our age. Daniel Boone would play with the Indian boys and learn hunting skills from their fathers. They taught Daniel Boone how to walk through the woods without leaving a trace. He could hide downwind at a pond and watch the wild animals without their knowing he was only a few feet away," said Kyle.

"That would have been awesome," exclaimed Dillon with wishful anticipation. "But I don't think we have much to see out here but squirrels and chipmunks," he said as he pointed to a squirrel that scampered past his feet. "The deer, bears and mountain lions have been gone a long time."

"I also heard that Daniel Boone got his first hunting rifle when he was twelve!" continued Kyle. "He was such a good hunter that his mother would let him go into the woods and shoot wild animals for their supper each day."

"I don't think my mother would ever let me go out hunting for food! I can hear her now: 'You will end up shootin' somebody!'" Dillon sighed. "Of course, things are a little different nowadays. You can't go into *town* with a rifle, shooting squirrels," he chuckled.

"Hey, there's the big oak tree that fell over the stream," said Dillon as he began to run towards it. "The big thunderstorm last year knocked it over when lightning hit it."

"Wow, that lightning split it right in two!"

"Yeah, and it pulled the roots right out of the ground!" added Dillon.

"Let's see if we can cross over it to the other side," challenged Kyle as he made his way to the foot of the log. "We'd better be careful though. We don't want to fall into the water and get wet!"

"Aw, I'm not worried about that. If Daniel Boone could do it, so can we!" said Dillon with confidence.

Soon the boys were cautiously walking over the fallen oak that led to the other side. They held both arms straight out from their sides to balance themselves. The water was trickling over the sandstones that were stained a chestnut brown by the minerals in the water.

The Lunchtime Mishap

They took one step at a time, careful to place one foot directly in front of the other so as not to step off the log. The most difficult part was at the other side, where the huge roots were sticking up in the air. They would prevent the boys from making an easy exit off the log.

"We're doing great! Now all we have to do is get around these roots," said Kyle.

The Big Hike

Kyle slipped one foot around the roots. With his foot moving out ahead of him, he began to slip. "Aghh!" he screamed as he began to fall backward into the stream. He quickly reached for the roots and grabbed them tight. He was now hanging on for dear life.

He glanced over toward Dillon who was standing wide-eyed and pale faced, frozen on that old log.

"Whatever you do, don't bump into *me!*" warned Dillon, as Kyle slowly worked his way around the crooked roots. "You're shaking the log! Be careful!" he said with a quivering voice.

Finally, Kyle made his way past the roots and placed both feet on solid ground. "Whew, that was a close one!"

"It may have been close for you, but I'm not there yet!" Dillon replied.

"Be careful, Dillon. Just grab that tall root, then swing your foot around."

Dillon carefully put his arms around the big root that stood straight into the air, then swung around it with a push from his right foot. Finally, he too was on the other side, and they both laughed in relief.

The Lunchtime Mishap

"I can just see you lying in the stream, all soaking wet," Dillon mused aloud as he began to roll on the ground with laughter. "You should have seen your face. Your eyes were as big as cupcakes!"

"I know. I thought I was a goner," said Kyle. As he turned away from the laughing Dillon, he noticed the big English walnut tree in the distance. "Well, if you are done laughing, we can go to the walnut tree and eat our lunch."

Dillon managed to pull himself off the ground but was still smiling from ear to ear. He let out a chuckle every so often as he reflected on Kyle's near disaster.

They walked down a path that led through the trees. Lining the path were trees such as oak, sugar maple, walnut and birch; then there was the large English walnut tree. It was a nice tree to eat under, for its large limbs sprawled out in all directions.

Its huge leaves were different from the leaves on the other trees. From its branches hung the yellowish-green walnuts that would soon be ready for gathering by the squirrels and stored in their winter dens in other trees.

The Lunchtime Mishap

The boys didn't say much as they ate their lunches. They were enjoying the wonderful day and the peaceful surroundings of the pond and trees.

"It sure is nice here," said Dillon. "You can just tell that a Creator designed everything around us."

"I know," said Kyle. "I think it's silly for people to believe that all these trees and animals got here by accident or that we came from mud puddles."

✖ ✖ ✖ ✖

Boys and girls, I think Kyle is right, don't you? It is difficult to think that we arrived on the planet by accident. Many believe that a big explosion took place to form our planet with all its wonder. The Bible tells us quite a different story. It says that God is the great Creator. It says that by God's wisdom the earth was created.

Did you ever think about how smart God must be to create the universe? This observation by Dillon and Kyle is a reminder of Proverbs 3:17–20. Let's read it together:

The Big Hike

"*Her ways are ways of pleasantness, and all her paths are peace.*

"*She is a tree of life to them that lay hold upon her: and happy is every one that retaineth her.*

"*The LORD by wisdom hath founded the earth; by understanding hath he established the heavens.*

"*By his knowledge the depths are broken up, and the clouds drop down the dew.*"

It says that God's wisdom is like the trees and pathways in our story. How is it similar? Just like a peaceful and beautiful outdoor path through the woods and around a pond or lake, so is living for God. Let me explain.

If you were to hike the Appalachian Trail in the eastern United States, you would come across various things. Since you might come across dangerous creatures and obstacles that could harm you, it would be good to have a guide along to point out where and what those dangers are.

The boys almost fell into the water because they had never crossed that log before. It was a lot easier for Dillon to cross safely because he listened to the advice of Kyle. Kyle learned the hard way because he had never done it. However, once he made it past the roots of the tree, he was able to guide Dillon around them safely. Since God knows all about the way we are taking, His Word is our guide through life.

Another thing that could happen to you is that you could get lost. The Appalachian Trail is marked so you know you are going the right way. The Bible is like that too. We can read it and find out whether or not we are going the right direction.

Living for God is also like a hike because it is full of delights and joys. There will be times with God that will be like mountaintop experiences, unequaled in beauty. When we trust God to lead us, we will find it to be just like that. He promises a peaceful journey for those who live for Him. Wonderful things come to those who love Jesus. Even when something bad happens or the journey gets hard, God is able to make it a blessing and benefit in our lives.

Dillon and Kyle's hiking path was lined with trees. When you take a walk in the forest, you see lots of trees. They are what make the walk unique. Did you know that life with God is lined with trees as well? He designed four types of trees that we will see in life.

First, trees for food. God designed many types of trees so we might be able to eat from them.

Second, trees for pleasantness. God made many of the trees just so we could enjoy their beauty. They also become homes for many birds and other creatures. It's fun to look at those things, isn't it?

Third, the tree of knowledge of good and evil. This was a tree that God made and placed in the Garden of Eden. He told Adam and Eve not to eat the fruit on that tree. If they did, they would die.

We know that they foolishly sinned against God. Then death was passed upon every person who has ever lived. That meant that unless God did something, we would die and never see Him again. We would be separated from Him forever in the lake of fire.

God did do something. He made another tree.

Fourth, the tree of life. A tree that gives

eternal life was to be found in the Garden of Eden (Genesis 2:9). It is in Heaven now (Revelation 22:2). However, we can have eternal life if we place our faith in the tree of Calvary where Jesus died for our sins and shed His blood so that we could be forgiven. That old rugged cross is our tree of eternal life.

Just like a person must take the fruit off a tree to enjoy it, you must take hold of eternal life by eating from the tree of life. You must pick of its fruit and eat it if you are to have eternal life.

How do you do that? By receiving Jesus as your Saviour. Look at what John 3:16 says:

"For God so loved the world, that he gave his only begotten Son, that whosoever believeth in him should not perish, but have everlasting life."

You reach out with a heart of belief. You accept the gift of eternal life by allowing Jesus to pay for your sins. If you have never done that, why not receive Jesus as your Saviour right now? Believing with all of your heart in Jesus as God's Son and the One who paid for your sin upon the cross, pray this simple prayer:

The Big Hike

Dear God, I know that I have sin in my heart. I know that because of that sin, I am separated from You. I believe that Jesus took my place by dying on the cross. He shed His blood and died for my sins. I believe that He is the true Saviour because He arose from the dead. I believe that Jesus will take me to Heaven if I trust Him. So I now trust Jesus to save me from Hell and to take me to Heaven when I die. I want Jesus to be Number One in my life. Thank You for saving me. Amen.

Kids, if God is smart enough to create the world and keep it running, don't you think He is smart enough to save you and to take you to Heaven when you die? Of course He can! Moreover, if God's knowledge can do such marvelous things, don't you think it would be a good idea to learn what He knows?

✖ ✖ ✖ ✖

Dillon and Kyle had a great lunch. Their stomachs were full of sandwiches, chips, cookies, juice and some Hershey's Kisses Dillon's mother stuck in their sacks.

"Wow, what a lunch!" exclaimed Dillon. "I

The Lunchtime Mishap

don't think I could eat any more, do you?"

"No way," Kyle replied. "I think those Hershey's Kisses finished me off! I feel like my stomach is going to burst wide open!"

"Mine too," said Dillon. "We'll probably look like a pair of penguins waddling down the path."

Both laughed as they began to put their things in the knapsacks. Then they slipped on their gear and were off to the pasture that belonged to a man known locally as Farmer Smith.

Chapter 6
Crosby's Surprise

Farmer Smith, as the children affection-ately called him, gave hayrides to the children each year at his farm. Mrs. Smith would fix hot cider and gingersnaps for them after the ride was over. Mr. Smith would arrange his barn into a straw maze from the straw bales that were neatly stacked inside. It was the highlight of October, and in just a few weeks, they would be on the nighttime tractor ride.

At other times of the year, they just liked walking through the tall pasture grass and climbing the fences from one field to the next. They especially liked to see the many farm animals grazing happily in the lazy days of summer—sheep, cows, horses and even a few pigs.

Dillon and Kyle couldn't resist skipping some stones across the local pond along the way. Kyle won the skipping contest, with fifteen skips of a stone in one toss.

They even frightened some of the ducks into flight when some of the stones came near them. The boys didn't mean to scare them; nonetheless, the ducks quacked angrily in protest as they flapped their wings and hurriedly paddled their webbed feet in order to lift themselves into the air.

After the pond fun was over, they headed up a narrow dirt pathway which led to the west and into the farmland beyond. The path was not used very often except for country travelers and local farmers.

The pair kept walking for about a mile, observing the scattering of various trees, wide-open farmland pastures and long stone fences. These were stacked by the farmers as they cleared rocks from the fields.

As they walked down the path, they could have gone in many directions but kept to the map. They had yet to explore all the areas, but they would have to do that another day. It was getting late, so they knew they couldn't get sidetracked.

"Hey, look over there," Dillon said as he pointed off to their right. The look on his face spelled adventure.

"Look over where?" asked Kyle.

"Over there!" Dillon said as he pointed with a more defined stretch and jerk of his arm.

Looking to his right, Kyle noticed a hand-made limestone wall sticking out of the grass with some black iron edging on top of it.

"I don't think I've ever seen that before," he said. "I know it's getting late, but we can at least take a quick look." Dillon didn't say a word, just turned on his heels and gave Kyle a slight push in that direction.

Soon they were walking through the high grass toward the stone wall. As they approached it, they could see that it was about two feet high. The wall made its way around to a large, rusty, black iron gate that stood about ten feet high.

"Kyle, let's see what it says on the gate."

They walked around to the front of the

fence and looked up at the large gate. Large letters also were formed out of iron; it read **CROSBY CEMETERY** across the top.

It seemed they read it at the same time, then both read it quietly. Their mouths dropped open in horror as they recognized where they were.

"Do you know where we are?" asked Dillon in a slow, frightened tone.

"I sure do. This is Crosby Cemetery!" Kyle said slowly.

"I've heard about it, but I've never seen it," Dillon said, still nervous.

The Crosby Cemetery was the oldest cemetery in the county. Legend had it that the Crosby family built the cemetery in the early 1800s for their teenage son, who was murdered. The parents buried him but never found the one who killed him.

Not only that, his body was supposed to have disappeared without a trace shortly after the burial. People claimed that his ghost walks through the cemetery and snatches boys and girls who get too near it.

Now, it is only a legend, but nonetheless it gave the boys some concern.

Crosby's Surprise

"Do you think all that stuff they say about it is true, I mean about the Crosby boy snatching boys and girls and all?" asked Kyle.

"I don't think so," replied Dillon. "I think grown-ups just made it up to scare us kids. Let's climb over the fence and look around."

"I don't know if I want to," protested Kyle. "Even if it isn't true, I don't know if I can stomach it."

The Big Hike

"Come on," challenged Dillon. "I dare you! You aren't a scaredy-cat, are you?"

Kyle wouldn't have been very happy to be labeled a scaredy-cat, especially by his best friend. Besides, Dillon was already straddling the fence and getting ready to swing his leg over.

"No, of course not!" he defied, valiantly. Deep inside he wasn't so sure of himself. He swallowed hard and jumped up on top of the fence wall and stood there for a moment, making sure nothing was in there before he took the final jump into the cemetery.

Dillon immediately began to look at the tombstones. "Hey, look here! It says,

Rebecca Crosby—born October 14, 1879/died June 4, 1960.

"She was about 80 years old when she died. Let's keep looking around and see if we can find that teenage boy's grave."

"Here's another one! It reads,

Charles Crosby—born 1803, died 1849,"

Kyle reported somberly. "He wasn't very old when he died. It has some more writing on it:

He went over there, to the streets of gold;

**for he was killed by a bear
before he was old."**

"That's a weird epitaph. It sounds like the bear got him before he got the bear," said Dillon.

Kyle asked skeptically, "Are you sure you want to do this? This place gives me the willies!"

"Just keep on looking," Dillon commanded. "I think his name was Billy Crosby. Here's another one over here."

Dillon headed toward an old oak tree, its branches crooked with age, standing tall in the middle of the cemetery. It looked like it would grab hold of you if you got too close to it.

"Hey, I bet it's over here. This tree must be about 150 years old," he said.

Even Dillon was getting a little quieter and looking somewhat frightened as he walked slowly toward the tree. Kyle was close behind him.

"Hey, there's an old white tombstone right there," said Kyle as he made his way over to Dillon.

Slowly and carefully, they walked toward the headstone in order to read the inscription. Dillon knelt down and pushed the

The Big Hike

overgrown weeds and grass away.

He began carefully reading the name—

William Crosby, age 17.

"This is the one! Billy must have just been his nickname. This is Billy Crosby's grave!" exclaimed Kyle nervously.

When he said that, they heard some of the bushes moving behind the old tree and saw the grass moving as someone came toward them through the bushes. Both were motionless with terror. Then they heard a loud squeal, "Eech!"

"Let's get out of here!" shouted Dillon with a squeal of his own.

It took but a moment for Kyle to turn on his heels and head for the stone wall. He hurdled rocks and tombstones to get out of there as fast as his legs could take him. Before he could get to the wall, he heard the voice of Dillon screaming at the top of his lungs, "Help, he's got me! He's got me!"

Kyle stopped, turned around and saw Dillon lying on the ground kicking and scratching the turf, trying unsuccessfully to go forward.

"He's got my leg! He's got my leg! Help!" Dillon screamed in horror.

Crosby's Surprise

Kyle reached down, grabbed a broken limb and turned back to save his friend. "Hold on, I'm coming!" he called.

Dillon kept screaming for help as his arms and legs moved frantically to get away. Kyle

was soon there ready to use the limb as a weapon, when he noticed a raccoon hightailing it for the stone wall.

Then Kyle dropped the limb and began to laugh at the top of his lungs. As he did so, he pointed towards Dillon's foot.

Dillon stopped screaming long enough to glance down at his foot. It was not a person at all but a root stump sticking out of the ground that had snagged his pants. Seeing that, he was more than relieved. He looked up at Kyle with a scowl and said, "It's not funny! I could have been killed!"

"Well, maybe, but I've never heard of anyone being killed by a raccoon. And besides, if you recall, you got a big laugh at me back at the stream," said Kyle as he continued to laugh uncontrollably.

Soon they were both laughing at the whole situation. In fact, the only one who wasn't laughing was the raccoon!

"I think we'd better get out of here before the real Billy shows up," suggested Kyle.

"I agree," said Dillon.

✖ ✖ ✖ ✖

Why did the boys get into their predicament? Wasn't it because they went into a cemetery that had troubles associated with it? When we go to places that aren't safe, we open ourselves to unnecessary problems and fears.

This story can teach us how we can avoid being afraid, or how we can avoid running into situations where we could get hurt.

First, the Bible tells us that we walk safely when we walk according to God's Word. It says in Proverbs 3:21,22:

"My son, let not them depart from thine eyes: keep sound wisdom and discretion:

"So shall they be life unto thy soul, and grace to thy neck."

The Bible shows us where the safe places are. It also warns us of dangerous things that can harm us. If we follow the Bible's instruction, we will be safe from evil because we will avoid dangerous situations and places.

When you are at play or with friends, don't let Bible principles depart from your eyes. Always remember to obey what it says and to apply it to every situation in life.

Also, in verse 23, it says that your foot will not stumble:

The Big Hike

"Then shalt thou walk in thy way safely, and thy foot shall not stumble."

Just like the tree root tripped Dillon, sin will trip us. This verse says that we won't stumble or trip over sinful things if we live by God's Word.

The word *stumble* also means "to stub your toe." If you have ever stubbed your toe on something, you know it can really hurt. The Bible tells us that even when you stub your toe on something in life, God will be there to help you stop hurting. He will be there to help you heal from it. There will be times you will have accidents or get into trouble. When something does trip you, God will get you back on your feet.

Second, we will sleep sweetly when we make God our confidence. Verses 24, 25 say this:

"When thou liest down, thou shalt not be afraid: yea, thou shalt lie down, and thy sleep shall be sweet.

"Be not afraid of sudden fear, neither of the desolation of the wicked, when it cometh."

Did you ever try to sleep at night but couldn't because you were too afraid of the dark? Maybe you thought there were monsters in your room or someone under your bed. Even though we know there are no such things as monsters, our minds tells us differently. Memorizing Bible verses can help you deal with your fears:

"The Lord is my light and my salvation; whom shall I fear? the Lord is the strength of my life; of whom shall I be afraid?"—Psalm 27:1.

"I will say of the Lord, He is my refuge and my fortress: my God; in him will I trust.

"Surely he shall deliver thee from the snare of the fowler, and from the noisome pestilence.

"He shall cover thee with his feathers, and under his wings shalt thou trust: his truth shall be thy shield and buckler.

"Thou shalt not be afraid for the terror by night; nor for the arrow that flieth by day;

"Nor for the pestilence that walketh in darkness; nor for the destruction that wasteth at noonday."—Psalm 91:2–6.

"He shall not be afraid of evil tidings: his heart is fixed, trusting in the Lord.

"His heart is established, he shall not be afraid, until he see his desire upon his enemies."—Psalm 112:7,8.

The Big Hike

"Say ye not, A confederacy, to all them to whom this people shall say, A confederacy; neither fear ye their fear, nor be afraid.

"Sanctify the LORD *of hosts himself; and let him be your fear, and let him be your dread."*—Isaiah 8:12,13.

When you fill your mind with lots of cold-blooded horror movies, you can't sleep well and you can't walk in dark places without fear. Instead of watching those things, why not read the Bible or watch things that are more wholesome? Why not go to church and think about the things of God?

Sometimes you can't sleep because you did something wrong and are trying to hide it. Even though it seems like you have gotten away with it, you feel guilty and worry that you will be caught.

When you do right, a peace comes into your heart; then you don't have to worry about the outcome that sin brings. When you go to bed at night, you can sleep well, for your mind is not full of worry and fear.

✖ ✖ ✖ ✖

Where were we in our story? Oh yes, I remember. "Raccoon or no raccoon, I'm not going back in that cemetery again!" stated Dillon firmly.

"Me either," agreed Kyle. "It's not worth sticking around to see if the real Billy Crosby is going to show up!"

Chapter 7
Smith's Pasture

The boys continued down the dirt road that eventually led into the pastures of Mr. Smith. He owned a lot of farm animals, including sheep, cows, horses, pigs, several types of fowl and many other animals normally found on a farm.

The first pasture they came to was outlined with a brown wooden fence that had been there for many years.

"Hey, there's the sheep pasture!" exclaimed Kyle. "It looks like the sheep are in there today."

Dillon and Kyle walked up to the fence to take a look. They placed their feet onto the first wide board of the fence while holding onto the top one with both hands. Looking all over the rich pasture, they noticed the sheep gently grazing on the plentiful grass. The sheep didn't pay much attention to the boys and continued to stuff themselves.

"Let's pay the sheep a little visit," suggested Dillon.

"Okay!" replied Kyle with a grin on his face.

As quick as a wink, they tossed their knap-

sacks to the ground and climbed over the fence. The sheep scattered in all directions. They ran to the far end of the field, keeping a close eye on the two intruders and wondering what the boys would do.

Dillon and Kyle sat on the ground and rested, watching the sheep. The sheep complained about the whole incident with a "ba-a-a." It sounded like they were saying "bad," as if to scold the boys for intruding.

"It must be nice to be able to wander around all day eating," said Kyle with a hint of envy.

"Yeah, they don't have to go to school or do any chores. All they have to do is stand around, eat and enjoy the outdoors. That's the life!" added Dillon.

"I'll say! All they really have to do is get a haircut once a year, and they are done," continued Kyle laughing.

"Let's go check out the cows," suggested Dillon. "I like to talk to them, don't you?"

"Yeah, they're funny. They just look at you like you're crazy," Kyle said with a chuckle.

Both rose to their feet and walked over to grab their knapsacks. Slinging them across

The Big Hike

their shoulders and onto their backs, they were off to visit the cow pasture just over the next hill.

It was relaxing to walk through the fields and feel the warm afternoon sun shining on their faces. They felt as if they could stay there all day long.

"I see the cows," Dillon reported as he pointed to the pasture before them. Most of the pasture was wide open, except for the outlining of fence rows which were covered in coats of honeysuckle and wild rose. The boys laid aside their knapsacks and used the crossovers to step over two of the fences into the cow pasture.

They began heading for the cows as they dodged sharp briars from the wild rose bushes that tried to snag their pant legs. When they got close enough to the cows, Kyle greeted them with, "Good afternoon, ladies, and how are you today?" (He had heard his dad say that many times and thought it sounded funny.) The black-and-white spotted cows pulled their heads up and looked at the boys, as they continued to take long, slow munches on the tasty pasture grass.

"What do you think of the weather?" Dillon asked. The cows just kept looking at them with a dumb expression. They seemed to enjoy the company of the two boys, even though they didn't understand a word they were saying.

After chatting with the cows for a few minutes, the boys noticed a large bull at the end of the pasture with his eyes fixed on the boys, closely watching their every move.

"There's the bull," said Dillon. "I wonder if he hates the color red, like the bulls in Mexico."

"I doubt it," answered Kyle. "I heard that those bulls are trained to hate the color red. He is probably as harmless as a kitten."

"Let's go meet him," Dillon suggested blissfully. He had begun to move toward the bull, with Kyle right beside him, when the animal started to paw the ground and snort. The boys stopped dead in their tracks.

"Hey, I don't think he's too friendly," Dillon judged, his voice quivering with each word.

"Do you think he will come after us?" inquired Kyle, who was equally worried.

"I think he might. We'd better start backing

out of here before he starts to charge."

Keeping their eyes glued on the bull, they began walking slowly backwards. The bull also kept his eyes on them as he continued to paw the ground and snort, with a shaking of his head from side to side.

Then the bull stopped his pawing and stood motionless for a moment. The three were staring each other in the eye. Then do you know what happened?

✖ ✖ ✖ ✖

Before I tell you, I want to share with you something about Proverbs, chapter 3. Verses 9,10 and 27 to 30 tell us something about farms, pastures and being a farmer, and they certainly relate to our story. Let's read those verses before we continue:

"*Honour the* LORD *with thy substance, and with the firstfruits of all thine increase:*

"*So shall thy barns be filled with plenty, and thy presses shall burst out with new wine.*"

"*Withhold not good from them to whom it is due, when it is in the power of thine hand to do it.*

"*Say not unto thy neighbour, Go, and come*

again, and to morrow I will give; when thou hast it by thee.

"Devise not evil against thy neighbour, seeing he dwelleth securely by thee.

"Strive not with a man without cause, if he have done thee no harm."

When I think of a farm, I think of a place that gives us many things. We receive milk and food, and a feast for the eyes as we enjoy a farm setting in the country.

Did you know that God designed everything in creation to give? What do I mean by that? Well, in this story we find different types of pastures. Each is there to give. Their entire purpose for existing is to feed the animals.

Do fields ever need to receive or take? Sure, they do. They take in sunshine and rain in order to produce grass. However, what is the main purpose of the field? To give. Taking is necessary to be able to give.

The sheep and cows likewise take in. However, they receive in order to fulfill their functions in life. They give of their wool or milk.

We too are to be givers. The Bible tells us that we are to live with an attitude of giving, not one of receiving. Paul quoted Jesus as

The Big Hike

saying that it is better to give than to receive. The important thing is not what others can do for us, but what we can do for others.

Happiness is not found by living only for ourselves. Happiness is something we find as we give ourselves to benefit others. We are not to live so that others can feed us, house us and take care of us; rather, we are to meet *their* needs.

In the Bible passage we just read from Proverbs 3, it tells us that there are four ways we can be givers.

First, when you have the power to help someone, do it, it says in verse 27.

Galatians 6:10 states:

"As we have therefore opportunity, let us do good unto all men, especially unto them who are of the household of faith."

In other words, if you have the ability to do good to others, do it. Our lives should be spent in doing good, not evil. We should work hard to help others in whatever way we can—shovel a sidewalk for an elderly person, clean the house for your busy mother, keep your bedroom clean, help with the dishes, take out the garbage, vacuum the floor or help your schoolteachers whenever you have the opportunity.

Second, give of yourself today. Verse 28 warns us not to say, "To morrow I will give." Do it the moment you have the opportunity.

Sometimes we may give the excuse that when we get older or perhaps when we have more time, we will give or help others. But God tells us not to put it off, for the opportunity may not come tomorrow.

Third, give kindness. Verses 29 and 30 say that we are not to devise evil against our neighbor or quarrel with him without a sufficient reason. In other words, don't purposely withhold your giving and helping of others in order to hurt someone.

Fourth, give to God. Verse 9 says, "Honour the LORD with thy substance, and with the firstfruits of all thine increase."

The word "honour" means to respect God with your "substance." Your substance is what you own or earn from a job. The Bible uses the illustration of a farm to teach us about giving.

The farmer would harvest his crops each year. It might have been wheat or corn. Then he was to take the "firstfruits"—or the first ten percent of his crop—and give it to God as an offering. Verse 10 promised God would bless them when they did.

Look at what the first churches were told to do in I Corinthians 16:2:

"Upon the first day of the week [Sunday] *let every one of you lay by him in store, as God hath prospered him, that there be no gatherings when I* [Paul] *come."*

These early Christians brought their offerings to the local church. The church then used that money to spread the gospel message.

We continue to give to God in the same way today. We take the first ten percent of what we receive and give it to God in the church, and then that money is used to carry out the work of God in reaching others for Jesus Christ.

When you think about it, you know that God is a Giver as well. He doesn't just sit in Heaven and wait for everyone to bring Him things, does He? No, He gives to us every day.

The greatest thing God has given to us is eternal life through Jesus Christ. Just like a pasture that is full of grass waiting for something to eat it, the eternal life God has provided is waiting for us to receive it. If you have never done that, you need to do it right now.

✖ ✖ ✖ ✖

To Dillon and Kyle, it seemed like time stood motionless for a moment as the bull's big eyes looked directly at the two boys. He stopped his pawing as he seemed to tense his muscles for a charge. Suddenly the bull began to run at full speed straight for the boys!

Dillon and Kyle turned around and began running as fast as their feet could take them. They made a beeline for the fence! The bull was charging with his head lowered and the breath of his nostrils snorting out his fury!

The boys knew if they didn't get across the fence in time, they would be goners! Dillon got to the fence first, climbed up one side and jumped over to the other. Kyle was not far behind as he grabbed hold of the top rail of the fence! The bull was headed right for Kyle's back when he hopped over the fence with a yank of his arms and one big leap. As he did, the bull's nose skimmed his foot and pushed him over the fence, head over heels! As Kyle went airborne, he loudly screamed out, "Ah-h-h-h!"

Dillon had tripped and was lying on his back when he saw Kyle going through the air like a cannonball and somehow making a complete

somersault before landing with a big thump in the high grass. The bull didn't stop until he slammed against the fence with his big head and two horns. They could hear the crack of the fence, but, fortunately, he didn't break through it!

Kyle just lay there on his stomach with a petrified look on his face, as he gasped for air. Dillon was staring at the bull in hopes that he wouldn't come through the fence.

The bull glared at the two daringly and boldly through the fence and snorted one more time as if to say, "That will teach you not to come into *my* pasture!"

Kyle rolled over onto his back and sat up. "Wow, that was a close one!" he said.

"Too close!" Dillon added in relief. He rolled up his fist and shook it at the bull as he said sarcastically to Kyle, "Why don't we go back in there and teach that old bull a lesson he won't forget?"

With that, the two boys began to laugh in relief. Dillon laughed again as he explained how it looked when Kyle flew through the air like a flying acrobat. They had fun mimicking the scene, while the bull remained near the fence, guarding it.

The Big Hike

They decided that it would be a lot safer if they got out of there and headed for Sherman's Woods. So grabbing their sacks, they said goodbye to "the ladies" and began walking toward the sun lowering in the west.

Chapter 8
Sherman's Woods

Just like Devil's Den, Sherman's Woods was named from the time of the Civil War—only it was the townspeople and not Dillon and Kyle who named it.

It seems that General Sherman of the Union Army made camp there for about a week. The little town was quite proud of that historic fact. That was probably because nothing really exciting ever happened there. To mark the site, a plaque was placed on the large bronze statue of General Sherman mounted proudly with a saber in his hand upon a fierce, thoroughbred horse. Not only was it interesting to view, it was fun to climb up on the statue and the cannon that rested near it.

This wooded area was a special place for Dillon and Kyle because it held an air of mystery and adventure within its boundaries. Just the thought of the Civil War excited both boys.

"I can almost see those soldiers walking around in here, can't you?" asked Kyle.

"Soldiers, where?" exclaimed Dillon as he turned his head to look everywhere at once.

"I don't mean real soldiers, silly. I mean, I can picture them in my mind," replied Kyle as he stared at Dillon in unbelief.

"Oh yeah, I know what you mean. To think that the real General Sherman and his men were in these very woods is pretty awesome!" said Dillon.

The boys continued into the woods. The local folks didn't visit it often. About the only ones who would come were the local boys. They liked to play Civil War in the woods as much as Dillon and Kyle.

"It's starting to get a little darker," said Dillon. "We probably have only another hour of daylight."

"I think you're right. We might have only enough time to visit the swing," added Kyle.

The swing was located in the woods over a deep gully which went through the middle of Sherman's Woods. During a thunderstorm, the gully would fill up with water and act like a stream. The boys could cross over the gully by swinging on a big, loose vine that hung off one of the trees. They had fun swinging back and forth from one side of the gully to the other and acting like Tarzan.

"There's the path to the swing!" shouted Kyle.

They came to a fork in the path. One prong of the fork led out of the woods, while the other led to the swing and the deep interior of the woods.

As they stood there, Dillon noticed something on one tree. "What's this?" he questioned.

"It's a...a...a...skull!" Kyle shrieked over a lump in his throat.

The boys didn't like the looks of this at all. Not only was there a cow's skull nailed to the tree, but there was a sign that read:

ENTER AT YOUR OWN RISK

"I wonder who nailed this here?" Kyle questioned.

"I don't know," answered Dillon. "Why don't we take a look?"

Neither was about to have someone take away the swing. They began to walk cautiously down the path, glancing from side to side, looking for anything that looked like trouble.

"Hey, I hear someone," whispered Kyle.

"Me too!" said Dillon as he also began to whisper. "Let's cut through the woods and take a look at who it is."

Dillon took the lead as he walked off the path and into the forest brush, careful not to break any sticks and make a noise. They hunched over and sneaked their way toward the voices.

"Snap!" went the sound of a stick. The noise seemed to travel through the woods like a loud firecracker. Dillon had stepped on a branch that lay hidden beneath some leaves.

"Be quiet!" said Kyle as he got down on his haunches as far as he could.

"I didn't do it on purpose," Dillon responded. "Come on."

The boys could hear talking, and it sounded like some other boys. There was a fallen tree right by the spot. They inched their way to the tree, then popped their eyes over it to take a peek.

To their surprise, they could see a gang of boys smoking cigarettes. It was a mean-looking group, and several of them had long hair. One really big guy with a crew cut had a tattoo on his arm and was wearing a shirt that said "kill" on it.

Dillon, looking over at Kyle, warned, "This is the Skull Gang. If they find us here, we're in real trouble!"

"I know. They are the meanest boys in town," replied Kyle. "Look at them smoking those cigarettes. We'd better get out of here before they find us and turn us into whipping posts."

As the two listened, they could hear the gang bragging about the trouble they had gotten into a few nights before. They were using lots of bad language and describing how they had broken into a grocery store.

"So that's who broke into Carl's Market," whispered Kyle in disbelief. "The police have been trying to find out who did it. Mr. Carl is still in the hospital."

"Yeah, he never did get a good look at them. Let's listen to what they are saying."

The Big Hike

The boys tried to be as quiet and camou-flaged as they could be, as the gang of boys continued their conversation.

"Man, we really fooled that old man, didn't we?" bragged one of the boys as he took a breath full of smoke.

"I'll say. The last thing I saw was him falling into the trash pile and then on the ground!" laughed another boy as he leaned back on a large rock and exhaled some smoke into the air. "Old Mr. Carl didn't even know what hit him!"

The boy looked like the leader and had an arrogant look on his face, as if to show every-one how tough he was.

"When are we going to split up the money?" asked another boy.

"We'll do it as soon as we leave," answered the leader.

"We have to tell the police," whispered Dillon. "Let's get out of here."

The boys lowered their heads behind the fallen tree and began to crawl in the opposite direction. When they did, Kyle stepped on a thick branch that snapped with a loud "crack." The gang of boys turned their heads with a startle. Their eyes took them right to Dillon and Kyle!

"Hey, look! There's someone in the bushes," shouted the leader. "Let's get 'em!"

Dillon and Kyle took off running like two deer in the wind. They were good at running in the woods and had had lots of practice, but they weren't sure they could outrun the gang. The Skulls were older and able to run faster. They were leaping over the fallen trees and gaining on them.

✖ ✖ ✖ ✖

Boys and girls, if you can wait a minute, I'll tell you exactly what happened. But, first, let me share something with you out of Proverbs, chapter 3, verses 31 through 35. Please read the verses with me:

"Envy thou not the oppressor, and choose none of his ways.

"For the froward is abomination to the LORD: but his secret is with the righteous.

"The curse of the LORD is in the house of the wicked: but he blesseth the habitation of the just.

"Surely he scorneth the scorners: but he

giveth grace unto the lowly.

"The wise shall inherit glory: but shame shall be the promotion of fools."

The word "righteous" means to live right, to act according to what the Bible says is right, and to avoid what God says is wrong.

After we decide to trust Jesus as our Saviour, then we need to follow Him as our Lord. That means that we are going to follow Jesus in what He tells us to do.

What does our Lord Jesus want us to do? He wants us to avoid living a sinful life, and He wants us to practice living right and behaving right.

The Bible teaches us that there are consequences for our actions. There is no such thing as "nothing will happen" if we do either right *or* wrong. The truth is, if we do right, we will reap certain things from God; if we do wrong, we will reap other things from God.

For instance, if you stick your finger in an electric outlet, you get shocked. If you put your hand in the fire, you get burned. If you eat good food, you will be healthy.

In verses 31 to 33 we see what harm will come if we live an unrighteous lifestyle.

Therefore, we should not envy that type of person. Don't look at the person living in sin and wish you could do as he does.

Why does God tell you not to envy sinners?

First, you will reap the curse of God. The word "curse" means that God will have bad things to say about you. If you read your Bible, you will notice the many times God said bad things about people who lived sinful lives.

King Ahab was one of those people. God said he was the most wicked king that ever lived. One of Jesus' disciples, named Judas, was called the "son of perdition." Another by the name of Korah was called a traitor against God. Cain, Abel's brother, was described as a murderer.

Second, you will make God sick. In verse 32 we read the word "abomination." The word means disgusting. It literally makes God sick in the stomach.

Do you think God is able to fellowship with us if we are making Him sick? Of course not. We need to live so that He is pleased with us and wants to be with us.

Third, sinfulness causes God to scorn

you. Verse 34 tells us that He will scorn the scorners.

A scorner is one who shows utter dislike for the things of God. A scorner mocks righteous living. In our story, the Skulls were scorning right behavior. They were proud of their sinfulness. Since they scorned God, He will scorn them. I don't know about you, but I don't want God to curse me, to scorn me or to be made sick by me.

Harmful things happen to those who live a sinful lifestyle, but good things happen when you choose to live a righteous lifestyle.

First, you will reap the blessing of God. The word "bless" means that God will say good things about you. He called Abraham "the friend of God." He called David "a man after mine own heart." He called Simon "Peter," which means "a rock." He called Moses a leader of His people. He called Samuel a gift from God.

I want the God of the universe to say good things about me and thereby guide my life and make good things happen to me. Do you want the same?

Second, you will cause God to cherish

you. In verse 32, the word "secret" is used. It means that He wants to be your close Friend. Just like Dillon and Kyle are best friends, we can have God as our best Friend. God says that if you will live a good life and walk with Him each day, He will share things with you that others will not receive. God wants to be your Friend. He wants to have special times alone with you. He will cherish you. He will consider your fellowship valuable and wonderful. It will be a time of showing you that He loves you.

Third, you will cause God to show kindness to you. The word "grace" in verse 34 has the idea of extending kindness to you. He rewards your behavior with kindness. Even when you do the wrong thing at times, God will not punish you as severely if He knows that you are trying to do right.

Are you living so that God will be pleased? If not, then surrender your life to Him today. Make Him the Lord of your life and actions. Do what He would have you do.

✖ ✖ ✖ ✖

If you remember, the gang of boys called the Skulls were chasing Dillon and Kyle through the thick woods. The boys were dodging branches and briars as they darted from one path to the next. Fortunately, they knew the woods very well and were heading toward a familiar hiding place close to the gully.

As they approached the gully area by the swing, both made a giant leap to the other side and landed squarely on their feet. It was quite a jump and made their knees buckle on impact. It was something they had done many times in the past, and they were pretty good at it. They sprang back up and were able to keep on going.

The gang were fast on their heels. All of a sudden the boys could hear screams. Dillon and Kyle stopped long enough to turn their heads around and see what it was. It was then that they saw every one of the Skulls in midair flight with eyes wide open as he soared headlong into the deep gully. Dillon and Kyle heard a "thump, thump, thump, thump" and the sounds of cracking branches as the pursuers landed in the bottom of the gully.

The boys watched as they saw their attackers disappear into the deep trench. Apparently they didn't know that it was there, and before they knew it, they went face first into the branches, mud and thorns that lay at the bottom.

The two smiled at each other as the gang members yelped with pain from the ditch. Pausing only for a moment, Dillon and Kyle took off running as fast as they could, not stopping until they got to their hiding place. It was a hut which was formed from a large bush that grew up into the air. The branches grew so long that they bent over to the out-side and formed a large circle. It was kind of like an igloo, except with leaves and branches. It had an opening on the side and was just large enough for them to climb into. It was hard to see the opening unless you knew it was there. Once they were inside, they could sit in the hollowed-out area of the bush and not be seen. It would be hard for anyone to find them in there.

"We'd better stay in here until things are clear," panted Dillon.

"Yeah, and let's hope they don't find us," replied Kyle.

Chapter 9
The Dome

Dillon and Kyle huddled in the hutlike hide-away they called the Dome. It seemed like hours since they left the Skull Gang wrenching with pain in the ditch by their vine swing. They tried to be as quiet as they could although it seemed their hearts would pound out of their chests. Like a big drumbeat each boy's heart thumped, and each heavy breath sounded out like a cannon.

"I hope they don't find us in here. I can't imagine what they would do to us if they did," whispered Dillon.

"I know. We heard what they did to Mr. Carl and everything. They know that if we tell

the police, they will be punished."

Dillon grabbed Kyle's arm to stop him from talking. "Quiet! I hear someone coming. Get down!" The boys got down with their stomachs pressed to the cool ground and with their heads close so they could whisper to each other.

"You guys look over in those trees, and Sam and I will check in these bushes," commanded the leader. "Whoever finds them, grab them and then give a shout."

"Okay," said another boy. "We'll grab them all right. Then we'll let 'em have it."

"Did you hear that?" whispered Kyle as he swallowed hard. "We'd better say a prayer." He had never been so scared in his life.

"Sh-h-h-h!" Dillon said as he poked him on the leg. "Say a prayer, but say it silently."

They bowed their heads and began to pray for God to protect them. They asked Him to help them stay hidden from the gang members and to allow them to get home safely.

They could hear the boys from the gang poking around the bushes and searching around their hut. It sounded as if they were poking sticks into the bushes to see if they could find them hiding. Dillon and Kyle were trusting God to help them not be seen through the shrubs and bushes of their hideout. They knew that this would be a real test for the Dome.

"You'd better come out," shouted one of the boys. "If you come out, we'll let you go safe."

"Yeah, we just want to be friends," said another with a chuckle.

Dillon and Kyle didn't believe a word of it and lay on the ground motionless. It was hard to be absolutely quiet when they were so afraid.

They could now hear someone just outside of the Dome poking the bushes around them. All of a sudden, a large stick poked through the branches and leaves of their hideout.

"Maybe they are in here," said one of the boys. Again the stick poked through and hit Kyle in the back. He couldn't help but let out a sound of pain.

"Argh!"

"Did you hear that?" asked the boy with the stick. "I think I hit something."

"No, I didn't hear anything. Poke in there again."

Again the stick came through the leaves

and came about one inch from Dillon's nose. "I think they might be in here," said the leader. "We know you're in there; so come on out," he demanded.

Dillon and Kyle realized they were in big trouble. They looked into each other's fearful eyes as the sweat formed beads on their foreheads. Dillon took his hand and put his pointer finger to his lips to tell Kyle not to say or do anything. Then he folded his hands to signal Kyle to pray.

Dillon remembered Proverbs 3, verses 24 through 26, that his father explained to him one evening while they read the Bible together:

"*When thou liest down, thou shalt not be afraid: yea, thou shalt lie down, and thy sleep shall be sweet.*

"*Be not afraid of sudden fear, neither of the desolation of the wicked, when it cometh.*

"*For the LORD shall be thy confidence, and shall keep thy foot from being taken.*"

✖✖✖✖

What exactly does that mean? How could that help Dillon and Kyle now?

The first thing his dad said was to make

The Big Hike

God your confidence. This verse was first written in the Hebrew language. The word "confidence" comes from a Hebrew word meaning "fat." His dad went on to explain that fat represents excess and plenty.

Usually when you see a fat cat or dog, you are probably thinking that he gets plenty to eat. In fact, he probably gets too much.

Fatness will give a person a sense of freedom from worry because he has plenty to eat. When a person has lots of food, he doesn't worry where his next meal will come from. He simply goes to the refrigerator or cupboard. His confidence is in the kitchen.

Fatness can also represent an abundance of trust in a person or thing. For instance, most of you don't worry about not having food to eat at suppertime. Why? Because your parents always have food for you. You have confidence in your parents that they will provide for you.

When a person has lots of money in the bank, he doesn't worry about how his bills will be paid. All he has to do is go to the bank when he needs more money. It is his confidence, his place of trust.

The Dome

The fat was seen when the children of Israel offered sacrifices for their sin. One of the first things they were to do before the animal was put on the altar was to remove the fat.

Leviticus 3:16 says, "All the fat is the LORD's." All of the fat on the animal was to be removed from the flesh and burned as a sacrifice to God. Removing the fat pictured God's people's putting their confidence and trust in Him, not in themselves. We are to offer our self-confidence to God by relying wholly upon Him.

The second thing Dillon's dad said about this verse was that when you put your confidence in God, the Lord would keep you from being "taken."

Maybe you have seen pictures of people stepping into a snare. An enemy sets the trap so that when someone puts his foot into the loop of the rope, the tree branch springs into the air and the person goes up with it, hanging him upside down by the foot.

Think of each snare as a sin or as an obstacle keeping you from living for God. The Devil is placing snares in our paths so we will get hung up. How do we avoid them? God shows us where they are as we put our confidence in Him and in His Word.

What if we don't listen to God and step into a snare laid by Satan? God said that He can show us a way to escape by trusting in His Word. Although sometimes He totally delivers us from the dilemma, God can also help us when we are *in* trouble. He has done it for many people throughout the years, and He can do it for you.

✖ ✖ ✖ ✖

Dillon thought about this as the gang members outside the Dome were about to discover them. Somehow, though, he felt at peace. He knew that God would help them in their dilemma. He said a silent prayer one more time that God would protect them and that if they were discovered, He would help them at that time. Whatever happened, Dillon was going to obey God.

As soon as Dillon finished, he heard someone calling to the two gang members, "Hey, Jim and Sam! They're over here! Hurry up! They're taking off!"

"Let's go!" said the leader.

Just like that, the two gang members took

off running toward the others, leaving Dillon and Kyle in the Dome.

"Can you believe it?" Kyle whispered.

"Yes, I can. God answered our prayers. I don't know who or what they are chasing, but now's the time for us to get out of here."

In a flash, the boys dropped their knapsacks, got up and began making their way out of the opening in the Dome. They took a quick look and didn't see anyone.

"It looks like the way is clear. Let's go!" commanded Dillon. "Just keep low and move as quickly and quietly as you can. Once we get to the clearing, we can run full speed back to your house."

They could still hear the gang in the distance, running through the woods in the wrong direction. Their voices got quieter and quieter as they moved farther away.

"There's the clearing; run like crazy," said Dillon.

They ran through the pasture and over the fence, then through another pasture. Still they could see no one following them. They ran across the bridge that led into town, and

down the streets toward Kyle's home, watching just in case any of the boys might be looking for them in town. They rounded the last corner to the street that led to Kyle's house.

"Hey, lookee there!" said Kyle, pointing down the street.

Dillon turned and watched as the Skull Gang members, each in handcuffs, were escorted by several police officers into the police station.

The sun was beginning to set, and it was becoming dusky when they reached the front porch of the house. They were panting as they plopped down on the steps of the wooden porch, huffing and puffing.

"Do you know what?" Kyle asked.

"No, what?"

"That was too close for comfort. I can't believe we got out of that one."

"That was close, all right, but God helped us get back safely. He answered our prayers."

"That's really awesome," Kyle said as he gave it some thought and began to smile. "We'll have to go back tomorrow afternoon and get our knapsacks from the Dome."

Just then, Kyle's mother stepped through

the door and onto the porch. "Well, boys, it's good to see you back. Did you have fun?"

"We sure did!" Kyle responded.

"Here is some iced tea, since it looks like you are pretty hot. Did you have any problems?"

Kyle looked over at Dillon with a big grin and said, "Yes, we had a few problems, but God looked out for us. In fact, everything turned out just fine."

"Yes, Mrs. Keyser, it was a day we won't soon forget," agreed Dillon with a big, big smile.

For a complete list of books available from the Sword of the Lord, write to Sword of the Lord Publishers, P. O. Box 1099, Murfreesboro, Tennessee 37133.

(800) 251-4100
(615) 893-6700
FAX (615) 848-6943
www.swordofthelord.com